The World of the World Leaf

Written by Summer Edward
Illustrated by Sayada Ramdial

Collins

The Wonder of the World plant

The Wonder of the World plant was first discovered in Madagascar, but it also grows in the Caribbean island of Trinidad, where Wygenia lives. Because roots grow from the sides of the leaves, a Wonder of the World plant can be grown by simply placing a leaf on top of the soil. Children sometimes place a leaf between the pages of a book just to see the roots grow. This marvellous plant needs little water and provides medicine for many types of illness. Its scientific name is *Kalanchoe pinnata*, and in some countries it's called "Miracle Leaf" or "Air Plant". Whatever you call it, it's sure to work wonders!

Trinidadian English

I'm Wygenia. On my island, we speak a language that's all our own, so you might not be familiar with it. I'm going to tell you about the time my grannie got sick and how my **mooma** and I helped her get better. I'll tell you exactly how it happened, using the exact words Mooma and Grannie used.

I stare out the window at the howling wind and rain.

In our kitchen, it is warm and bright. Spicy-sweet cloves simmer in hot honey water.

"Carry some for Grannie," Mooma says. "To help with the **bad feeling**."

Grannie's room is quiet, the curtains pulled shut. I help her sit up and sip the warm tea.

"Thank you, dearie, that helps," Grannie says.

Grannie tries to smile but her head hurts. Ever since Grandad passed on, she hardly talks and lies in bed a lot.

In school, it's hard to pay attention. We are learning about a plant called Wonder of the World. Everyone gets a leaf to put inside their copybook.

"This is a very special leaf," **Miss** says. "It can grow into a new plant, just like a seed."

Miss teaches us about **bush medicine**. "Long ago, plants like Wonder of the World were used to help sick people get better."

After school, I show Mooma my leaf.

"What you know 'bout Wonder of the World, chile?" Mooma says, chuckling. "That is thing from before time."

"It could cure sick people like Grannie," I say.

"Well it might work," Mooma says. "But you need plenty of leaves."

On Sunday, Mooma and I drive to Mount St Benedict, an old abbey in the hills. Below, the streets and houses of our island look tiny.

Inside the cool quiet abbey, Mooma and I light candles and say a prayer for Grannie.

On the way back to the car, we pass a plant shop.

"Mooma, you think they does sell Wonder of the World plants there?"

"Let's see," Mooma says.

The plant man is Mooma's friend, Mr Bailey. I tell him we need a Wonder of the World plant to make bush medicine for Grannie.

Mr Bailey looks, but doesn't find any.

"Those plants hard to find nowadays yes," he says, scratching his head.

"**Don't mind that**," Mooma says, rubbing my back. "At least we tried."

Later, my neighbour Sanjay comes over. I tell him I tried to find a Wonder of the World plant for Grannie.

"Ent the leaves does grow like a seed?" Sanjay says. "Let we plant ours and see what go happen." What a great idea!

We take the leaves from our copybooks and place them under the lime tree.

Sanjay grins. "Just now we go have a whole plant!"

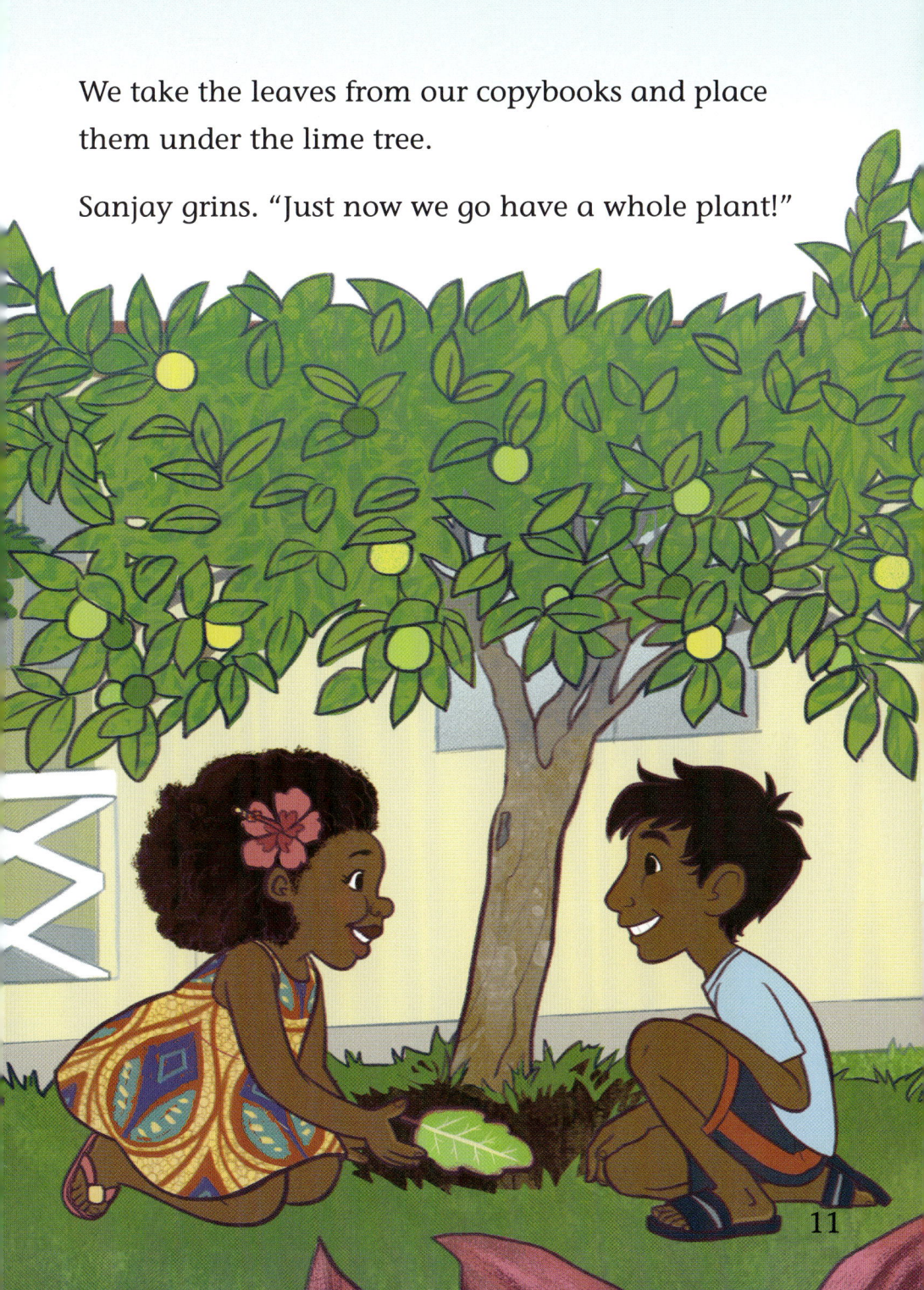

That night, I take Grannie her favourite dinner, **crix** and **buljol**, but she isn't hungry. I tell Grannie about my plan to make bush medicine.

"Bush medicine can't cure everything," Grannie says, closing her eyes. "It won't work."

"But it might help," I say, trying not to cry.

Grannie looks sad. I feel lonely.

"Please, Grannie," I beg. "You don't want to get better?"

Grannie finally opens her eyes and looks at me. "OK, Wy-Wy," she says, hugging me. "I will try it, but I only doing it for you."

Every day, Sanjay and I water the soil under the lime tree. Soon, tiny shoots begin poking up.

"**Whey**! This plant growing fast!" Sanjay says.

Weeks pass. Two stems with big leaves rise into the air.

One day, Mooma inspects our plants.

"I think it ready yes," she says. Finally! "Pick two leaves and bring them, Wygenia."

In the kitchen, Mooma soaks the leaves in boiling water to make tea. I wait anxiously as Grannie takes a sip.

"Not bad," Grannie says. "Thank you, **doux-doux**."

Days go by. Grannie drinks more tea and says she feels a little better, but I'm not so sure.

Sanjay's **aja** peers through our fence. He knows that Grannie isn't feeling well. "You try a **tie-head**?" he asks. "That does work."

That night, Mooma rubs **sof' candle** onto a Wonder of the World leaf and warms it over a candle's flame. She wraps a cloth, with the greasy leaf inside it, around Grannie's forehead.

"How the tie-head feeling, Grannie?"

"Warm," Grannie says. "And nice."

On Saturday, Sanjay and his aja come over. We sit in the **gallery** and eat **benne balls**. The pawpaw tree dances in the breeze as Aja talks about the old days.

Grannie listens quietly and sips Wonder of the World tea.

"We having a tea party," Sanjay laughs.

"You mean a tea **lime**!" Aja says.

"I feel this tea working yes," Grannie says.

"We should do this every weekend!" I say.

So we do. Every weekend, throughout the dry season, we have the tea lime. Soon all the neighbours know about it. They wave to Grannie and wish her good health.

"Story time!" I say, when the sun goes down and shadows fill the yard.

Then Aja tells us tales about the **jinn**, **Papa Bois**, and **Anansi** the tricky spider, who live in the forests. Grannie listens too and smiles. Soon, she feels stronger. Her eyes glow brighter and her head stops hurting.

One day, Grannie visits the doctor. I try to play jacks, but I'm too nervous to remember my count. Suddenly, the door opens and there is Grannie, leaning on Mooma's arm.

"Everything good," Grannie says, smiling. "The doctor say I going and be OK."

"Hurray!" I shout.

While I do a victory dance, Mooma talks on the phone.

"That was Mr Bailey," Mooma says. "They planting a garden on the Mount tomorrow. I told him we would help."

This time, Grannie drives up to the Mount with us. Blooming poui trees fill the hills with bright colours. Sanjay, his aja, and lots of other people have come out to help plant the garden.

"Today we will plant lots of different plants that can help sick people in our community get better," Mr Bailey tells everyone.

"Wonder of the World too?" I ask.

"Certainly!"

Everybody gets a trowel. Even Grannie digs a little. Afterwards, Daddy and I hand out **currant rolls** and **nut cakes**. Our neighbours give Grannie gifts.

fever grass

vervine

cat's claw

shining bush

"Three cheers for Wygenia!" Mr Bailey says. "I got the idea to grow this garden after she told me about the Wonder of the World plant."

Everyone smiles at me and claps. I feel proud. Suddenly, the rain begins to drizzle although it's still sunny.

"Well, **I never see more!**" I exclaim, lifting my hands in wonder. Everybody laughs.

"**I eh able with you yes!**" Grannie says, laughing hardest of all.

I haven't heard Grannie laugh in a long time.

Grannie kisses my forehead. "Now I really feel better," she says. "Thank you, Wygenia."

Glossary of Trinbagonian terms

aja an Indian word that means "grandpa" or "grandfather"

Anansi a half-spider, half-man trickster who is a central character in Caribbean folklore

bad feeling an unwell or nauseous feeling, especially a stomach ache

benne balls Trinbagonian sweets made from sesame seeds, spices and sugar syrup, rolled into balls

buljol salted cod with oil, fresh peppers, tomatoes, onions, cucumbers and sometimes boiled eggs

bush medicine plants and seeds used to cure sick people; a doctor who uses bush medicine is called a bush doctor

crix a type of Trinidadian cracker

currant rolls flaky Trinbagonian pastries containing a filling of currants and sugar

don't mind that don't worry about it

doux-doux	sweetheart
gallery	the patio or porch of a house
I eh able with you yes!	a phrase which expresses amusement at someone's entertaining behaviour
I never see more!	an expression of surprise, astonishment or disbelief
jinn	ugly and evil demons in Indo-Caribbean folklore
lime	an informal social gathering
Miss	how Trinbagonian children address their female teachers
mooma	mummy, mother
Papa Bois	Father of the Woods, a character in Trinidadian folklore, pictured as an old man with cloven hooves instead of feet
nut cakes	Trinbagonian sweets made from peanuts, sugar syrup and ginger
sof' candle	whale fat used for medicinal purposes
tie-head	a piece of cloth tied around the head in combination with a salve of herbs (rosemary, bay leaf, coconut oil, etc), commonly worn for headaches
whey!	expression showing shock or surprise

How is Wygenia feeling?

Distracted – "In school, it's hard to pay attention."

Disappointed – "Don't mind that," Mooma says, rubbing my back. "At least we tried."

Excited – What a great idea!

**Sad – "But it might help,"
I say, trying not to cry.**

Happy – "Hurray!" I shout.

Ideas for reading

Written by Christine Whitney
Primary Literacy Consultant

Reading objectives:
- read for a range of purposes
- make inferences on the basis of what is being said and done
- retrieve information from non-fiction

Spoken language objectives:
- ask relevant questions
- speculate, imagine and explore ideas through talk
- participate in discussions

Curriculum links: Science – use the local environment to explore plants growing in their habitat; Writing – narratives about personal experiences and those of others, write for different purposes

Word count: 1075

Interest words: bush medicine, abbey, anxiously, distracted, gallery

Resources: ICT for research; paper, pencils and crayons; a selection of Trinbagonian fruits for tasting and plants for observing

Build a context for reading

- Ask children what they know about the following foods: *buljol, benne balls, currant rolls, nut cakes*. Have they ever eaten any of these?
- What do children understand by the phrase *bush medicine*? Have they heard of a Wonder of the World leaf?

Understand and apply reading strategies

- Read up to the end of p9. What is happening in Wygenia's family? Why have Wygenia and her mooma driven out to the abbey?
- Continue to read to p15. Ask children to discuss how Wygenia is feeling and to find words that show this.
- Continue to read to p21. Ask children to talk about the stories that are told as the family and neighbours gather in the gallery. They might talk about the tales of the *jinn, Papa Bois* and *Anansi*.

Develop reading and language comprehension

- Ask children to read pp22–27 and to discuss how the reader knows that Grannie is feeling better.
- On p25, the neighbours plant lots of different plants. These are medicinal plants they have brought from their own gardens, such as: *vervine, shining bush, Aloe vera, fever grass, cat's claw* and *Senna*. Ask children to research these plants and what they are used for.
- Read pp30–31. Read the words: *distracted, disappointed, excited, sad, happy*. Ask children to talk about how Wygenia's emotions change throughout the story using these words to help them. Could they find illustrations from the book that show how she is feeling?

Support a creative response

- Using their knowledge about the medicinal plants given to Grannie, ask children to produce a fact-file of information and drawings of these plants.
- Set up a tasting centre in the classroom and enjoy some of the foods mentioned in this story.
- Suggest to children that they try growing a Wonder of the World plant. They could keep a record of its growth and write a recipe for its medicinal use.

Read more

The Jungle Outside (Lime/Band 11) is a story about exploring the wonders of nature in a garden in the Caribbean.

White
Band 10

The Wonder of the World Leaf

When her Grannie falls ill, Wygenia hopes that the Wonder of the World plant can make her better. But will it work?

ISBN 978-0-00-841388-0

A Caribbean story

www.collins.co.uk/collinsbigcat